THE SURPRISING WORLD OF
Plants

Written by Helen Strahinich

STECK-VAUGHN
A Harcourt Company

www.steck-vaughn.com

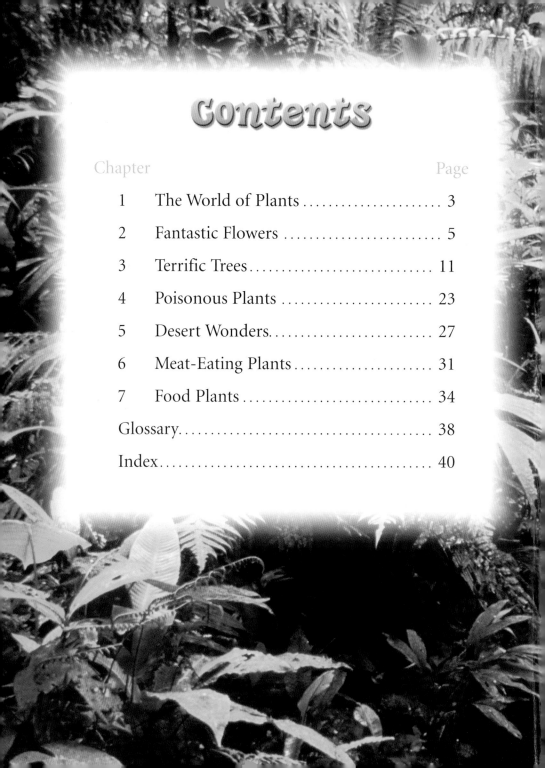

Contents

Chapter		Page
1	The World of Plants	3
2	Fantastic Flowers	5
3	Terrific Trees	11
4	Poisonous Plants	23
5	Desert Wonders	27
6	Meat-Eating Plants	31
7	Food Plants	34
	Glossary	38
	Index	40

Chapter 1
THE WORLD OF PLANTS

About 300,000 different kinds of plants grow on Earth. They come in many sizes, shapes, and colors. Some are taller than the length of three football fields. Others are too small for you to see.

The needs of most plants are simple: soil, water, sunlight, air, and a few **minerals**. Like animals, plants use food to grow. They **reproduce,** creating more plants. But plants differ from animals in two ways. First, after they take root, most plants stay in one place their whole life. Second, most plants make their own food.

Plants vary greatly, but most plants have four important parts—roots, stems, leaves, and flowers. Roots hold the plant in soil, keeping it in place. Root hairs suck up water and minerals in the soil. Then the roots carry these things to the stem. The stem carries water and other materials up into the plant. The stem also supports the plant's leaves and flowers.

Leaves are a plant's food factories. To make food, leaves use sunlight, water, and carbon dioxide (a gas in the air). This process is called **photosynthesis**. A plant stores some of the food it makes. It also uses some of the food right away. A plant also gets rid of its wastes through its leaves. Later the plant sheds the leaves.

Flowers make seeds that can grow into new plants. To make seeds, many flowers need the help of insects and birds. These creatures are attracted by flower colors and smells. Some flowers give off a sweet perfume. Others smell like a dead animal.

Without plants little life could exist on Earth. Many animals eat plants. Other animals eat plant-eating animals. Either way, food chains begin with plants. Cattle and chickens, for example, eat plants. Meat-eaters consume beef and chicken. Without plants, there would be no cattle or chickens—and very few other living things.

Chapter 2
FANTASTIC FLOWERS

About 250,000 types of plants grow flowers. All flowers have the same important job—to make seeds that can grow into more plants. The titan arum makes what has been called the world's largest, smelliest flower. It can reach 9 feet (2.7 meters) tall and 4 feet (1.2 meters) wide. The flower has an awful odor that smells like rotting meat.

The flower of the titan arum buds from a swollen underground stem. First, the new bud rests for a few days. Then it grows several inches per day. In full bloom, the titan arum gives off its rotten smell. If all goes well, the giant bloom collapses, and seeds form in thousands of berries inside the fallen plant. These bright red berries are the size of cherries.

The titan arum is very rare. In nature it grows only on one island in Southeast Asia. However, in 1999, a titan arum flowered at a special garden in California.

The plant was on view there for 19 days. During that time 76,000 people came to see the flower.

New plants grow from seeds inside the titan arum berries. At first each seed produces a leaf. This leaf looks like a small tree with an umbrella on top. The leaf may reach 20 feet (6 meters) in height. It won't produce a flower for seven years.

How do plants make seeds? Stamens in a flower make something called **pollen**—and lots of it. Grains of pollen are as small as specks of dust.

A titan arum plant in bloom

Flower Parts

Sepals protect the bud, or baby flower. As the petals grow, they push out the sepals. Petals protect the stamens and pistil inside. The pistil is the female part. Stamens are the male parts.

pollen

stamen

petal

pistil

sepal

receptacle

Pollen from the stamen must reach the pistil. Only then can the pistil make seeds. The pistil accepts only pollen from its own **species**. It ignores pollen from other kinds of plants. For most flowering plants, the pollen of one plant's stamens must travel to the pistil of another plant. However, a few plants can pollinate themselves.

How does the pollen get from a stamen to a pistil? **Pollination** happens in many different ways. Wind carries the pollen of many plants. Water does, too. Insects, birds, and other animals also carry pollen.

Some orchids (AWR kidz) have a special way of attracting insects. The flower of the mirror orchid has a blue patch that looks like the wings of a female bee.

When the male bee comes for a visit, part of the orchid snaps forward. It leaves grains of pollen on the bee. If the bee lands on another mirror orchid—wham! The pistil of the next flower picks up the pollen from the bee.

Each type of orchid attracts only one type of insect for pollination. The most famous orchid is the foot-and-a-half orchid. The foot-and-a-half-orchid flower has very long tubes that hold its **nectar**. This orchid's matching insect is a moth with a very long feeding tube. Only that moth can collect the nectar—and pollinate the orchid.

Some orchids lure their pollinators inside and trap them for a little while. As the insects are trying to escape, they are brushed with pollen. Bucket orchids are one example of orchids that

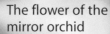
The flower of the mirror orchid

lure and trap insects. In Central America's rain forest, the upper leaves and branches of the tallest trees form a giant covering called the **canopy**. The canopy receives a lot of sunlight, so many plants, including bucket orchids, live there.

There are about 20 kinds of bucket orchids. Each kind has perfumed oil that attracts a certain kind of male bee. The bees need this oil to attract their mate. As the male bee moves toward the oil, it slips. Then it falls into a pool of the stuff. The bee has only one way out—through a tunnel. His back touches the tunnel roof, and pollen rubs off on him. When he leaves, the male is carrying pollen on his back. He's ready to pollinate another bucket orchid.

How do orchids and other plants get to the canopy? Some plants climb trees toward the sunlight. They use roots, stems, or even leaves to inch their way up. Once orchids are high in the trees, they use their root hairs to absorb moisture from the air. They also use their root hairs to absorb nutrients from decayed leaves in the canopy.

Other flowering plants called bromeliads (bruh MEE lee adz) travel to the sunny canopy as tiny seeds.

The wind carries them up. These plants wrap their roots around branches of trees for support. Their long leaves form cups. These cups hold water for the plant. Small creatures, such as frogs, insects, and even tiny snakes live in these little plant ponds. The creatures' droppings provide nourishment for the plant.

A flower stalk grows from the center of the cup. Seeds produced in these flowers may grow into new plants. Baby bromeliads may also sprout from the base of the mother plant. Baby bromeliads are called pups.

A bromeliad growing on a tree branch

Chapter 3
TERRIFIC TREES

Trees are the biggest plants in the world. To be called a tree, a plant must have one sturdy stem. This stem is known as a trunk. To be called a tree, a plant must also grow to a height of 20 feet (6 meters) or more. Trees can be divided into two groups called **conifers** and **broadleaf trees**. Both kinds make seeds.

Conifers

Conifers are cone-bearing trees. Pines, firs, and redwoods are all conifers. The cones hold and protect the tree's seeds. Most conifers have leaves shaped like needles. They shed the needles little by little, so the trees stay green all year. Because they stay green year round, conifers are called evergreen trees.

Conifers grow in a cone shape. This shape keeps snow from building up and damaging the tree. Conifers are hardy trees and are very **fragrant**.

The largest living things on Earth are conifers called giant sequoias (si KWOY uhz). Even though they are the largest trees, each one starts from a seed the size of a grain of wheat. The cone of a giant sequoia is the size of a chicken egg. In one year, an adult tree can produce 2000 cones that hold 500,000 seeds.

Some giant sequoias are so unusual that they have their own name. Each of these trees has enough wood to build 40 five-room houses. Each tree weighs about 6000 pounds (2727 kilograms) and is as tall as the Statue of Liberty.

Famous Giant Sequoias

Tree Name	Height	Distance Around	Age
General Sherman	290 feet (88 meters)	80 feet (24 meters)	2,250 years
General Grant	270 feet (82 meters)	107 feet (33 meters)	1,750 years

EXTRA! EXTRA!

ANNA MEHLIG CRASHES

On March 30, 2000, visitors at Sequoia National Park in California reported a huge crash. The cause? A giant sequoia named Anna Mehlig had fallen. Anna Mehlig stood near two other sequoias called Mother and Son, and Wooster. The last time a big sequoia tree fell in the park was 1965.

Bristlecone pines live even longer than sequoias, but they do not grow to be very tall because they live in a very harsh **environment**. Bristlecones grow on dry, windy mountaintops. Their trunks are twisted and bent. Much of the thick bark falls off. Only the green needles on some branches show that the trees are still alive.

How do scientists measure the age of these very old trees? They use an instrument called a borer. With the borer, they slowly dig a hole in the trunk. Then the scientists take out a thin sample of the trunk. The sample shows the tree's rings. Each ring stands for one year of the tree's life.

A bristlecone pine tree in the mountains of California

13

Broadleaf Trees

Broadleaf trees don't have needles. Instead, they have flat leaves. Most broadleaf trees shed their leaves at the end of summer. Examples include maple, birch, ash, aspen, and oak. These broadleaf trees are common throughout the United States.

Oaks have been called the lords of the forest. A full-grown oak tree is an acorn factory. It makes 90,000 acorns in one year and can make millions of acorns over its lifetime. Acorns are actually nuts. Each acorn holds a seed along with food that the sprouting seed can use. Acorns are important in the forest food chain. Birds, squirrels, deer, and other plant-eating animals dine on acorns. Then meat-eating animals such as foxes and owls eat the plant-eaters. Many animals often live in one oak tree. Insects munch the oak tree's leaves. Birds and bats feast on the insects that live in the oak. An oak tree may be home to 30 bird species, 200 moth species and 45 other insect species.

Squirrels and oaks are important to each other. Squirrels depend on the trees for food. In turn, squirrels do a job for the trees. Because squirrels can't eat all the acorns they find, they dig holes in the ground to store the ones they don't eat. Squirrels don't remember where they hide every acorn. The forgotten acorns sprout in warm weather and become oak trees.

If a baby oak tree grows too close to its parent tree, it probably will not get enough water, light, or minerals.

Squirrels eat some acorns and store others to eat in the winter.

Luckily, squirrels often hide acorns away from parent trees. If these acorns sprout, they have a better chance of getting the things they need to live.

Durian (DUHR ee uhn) trees grow in Southeast Asia. Durian trees live to ripe old ages—up to 150

❧ How Seeds Are Spread ❧

- Many seeds have special parts that give them a boost. Maple seeds, for example, have wings that spin as the seeds drop toward the ground. The wings make the seeds look like tiny helicopters. Kapok (KAY pahk) seeds have threads that float in the air. The wind may carry the seeds for miles.

- Mangrove seeds sprout on the parent plants. Then moving water carries off the sprout.

- Many kinds of animals spread seeds. For example, monkeys, antelopes, and elephants feed on the fruit of baobab (BAY oh bahb) tree. The animals eat some of the seeds with the fruit. Later they leave the seeds in their droppings.

years. They can reach heights of 150 feet (46 meters). There are many kinds of durian trees. One kind of durian tree makes a fruit that is bigger than a football. A durian tree's fruit is supposed to get better as the tree ages. Some people say that durian fruit tastes and smells wonderful. Others think it smells like a skunk! Either way, the durian fruit's smell attracts many animals from far away. Birds, squirrels, deer, bears, and monkeys soon come calling.

Tough Places for Trees to Grow

Trees grow just about every place on Earth. Hot, dry deserts have trees. Muddy swamps have trees, too. Trees make their home on mountain slopes. They also live on cold plains in the Far North. Only the South Pole has no trees at all. Temperatures there drop far below freezing, so none are able to grow. How do trees manage to grow in places like deserts and swamps?

Over time roots, trunks, leaves, and other tree parts have changed to **adapt** to their environment. These changes make it possible for some trees to live in places with extreme heat or cold. Other trees have changed to adapt to soggy or rocky areas.

Plants need water, but too much water or a great deal of salt kills most plants. Mangroves, however, live in salty, watery places. In watery areas the soil is so thick and muddy that it doesn't hold up most trees. Arched roots give a mangrove tree support and make the tree look like it is standing on stilts! The part of the root that is above water takes in air, while the rest of the root lies under water and mud. The deepest part of a mangrove's root is shaped like a spike to hold the tree in mud. Mangrove seeds grow roots while still attached to the parent. The root that grows from a seed may become fixed in the mud before the fruit falls from the tree.

How can mangroves live in saltwater? Some kinds of mangrove trees carry the salt to their leaves, which drop off once they are filled with salt. Other kinds of mangroves simply sweat the salt from their leaves.

Many creatures depend on mangroves. Seabirds nest in their upper branches. Fish, crabs, and other water animals live on or around their roots.

Unlike mangroves, other trees are suited to hot, dry lands. Both the baobab tree and acacia (uk KAY shuh) tree grow on the plains of Africa. These places have long dry seasons. Baobab trees get water during the short rainy season and then store this water in their wide trunk. They use this stored water when it's needed.

Baobabs live a long time—up to 3000 years! At about 20 years of age, they bloom for the first time. Their giant flowers are white and very smelly. Bats and insects come to the flowers in search of nectar. After pollination, big hairy **pods** form on the tree. These pods hold the baobab's many seeds.

A mangrove forest in Australia

Squirrels, snakes, insects, and birds live in baobab trees. All the parts of the baobab tree have been put to use by people, too. People use the trunks of baobabs for building houses and barns. The bark of the baobab is used to make rope, baskets, nets, and cloth. The roots have been used to make refreshing drinks, and the leaves have been cooked into soups.

Acacia trees have nasty thorns that keep away most of the animals that try to eat their leaves and roots. Giraffes, however, have tongues like leather. The thorns

Baobab trees grow to be about 50 feet (18 meters) tall.

don't hurt them. Some kinds of acacia trees give off a bad taste, so giraffes don't bother them.

Unfortunately, acacia thorns don't keep away leaf-eating insects. But acacias have a way of dealing with these pests, too. Special ants eat sap from the tree. These same ants fight off other insects. The ants don't bother bees that are needed to pollinate the acacia tree. The bees arrive at the hottest time of the day. That's when the ants are napping.

Acacias and baobabs survive in hot climates, but other trees have adapted to cold ones. The dwarf willow survives in the low temperatures and short summers of the Far North. This Arctic survivor is the shortest tree of all. Instead of growing straight and tall, the dwarf willow grows wide and low to the ground so that the wind can't blow it over. For added protection dwarf willows grow close together.

The gingko tree is a different kind of survivor. It has been on Earth for more than 200 million years. Charles Darwin, a famous scientist, called the gingko tree a living fossil because this tree has hardly changed over millions of years. The shape of the gingko leaf is very unusual. The leaf is shaped like a small green fan.

No other kind of tree anywhere has a leaf of this shape. *Gingko* means "silver apricot" in Japanese, after the fruit it bears. The gingko tree can survive in spite of disease, pollution, and pests. For this reason, gingkoes are found in many cities around the world.

Gingkoes are also known as **medicinal** plants. The Chinese first used gingko leaves as medicine about 2200 years ago. Different parts of the gingko tree are used to treat blood, memory, and lung problems.

Gingko leaves

Chapter 4
POISONOUS PLANTS

Plants have many ways to attract animals that will pollinate their flowers or spread their seeds. Many plants also have ways of protecting themselves against pests.

Some plants have thorns or sharp edges. Some grow needles or barbs. These growths can cut, prick, or stab unwanted visitors. The leaves or bark of some plants tastes bad to insects. Still other plants, such as the upas (YOO puhs) tree, defend themselves with poison.

The upas grows in Southeast Asia. One of its names is "the poison tree." The people of Java once used poison from the tree's bark on their arrows. It was useful for hunting or for defending themselves from enemies.

In the 1780s, Europeans living in Java made up stories about upas trees. They said that no creature could live within 18 miles (33 kilometers) of a upas tree. Only one in ten survived a visit to a upas tree, or so the story went.

The leaves of poison ivy grow in groups of three.

Touching some poisonous plants can sometimes bring on a nasty rash. Poison ivy grows in many parts of North America, Europe, and Asia. Its leaves produce a poisonous juice. Many people are sensitive to the juice. For these people, touching poison ivy causes a rash or swelling. Being able to recognize poison ivy is a skill that helps people stay away from it.

Another common plant with poison is milkweed. The plant's name comes from its milky juice. It oozes out of broken stems and leaves. The juice can cause a heart attack in small animals.

Monarch butterflies lay their eggs on milkweed plants. After four or five days, the eggs hatch as caterpillars. As the caterpillars eat the milkweed leaves, they store milkweed poison in their body. Because the poison tastes bad, **predators** leave the caterpillars alone. Later, when caterpillars change into butterflies, they continue to carry the milkweed poison in their bodies. Birds learn to recognize monarch butterflies and leave them alone.

In spite of the milkweed's poison, some people who are experts on milkweed collect its roots. They use small amounts to treat health problems. Poison ivy leaves have medicinal uses, too. For example, some people have used them to treat skin and joint problems.

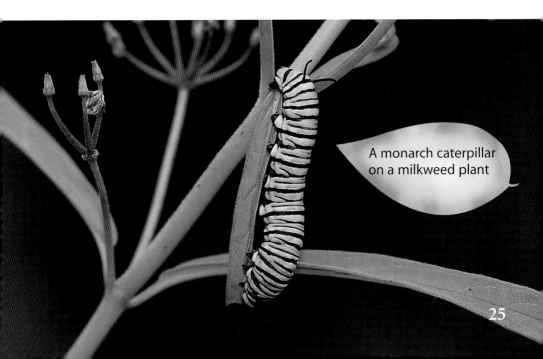

A monarch caterpillar on a milkweed plant

Plant Parts That Are Poisonous in Large Amounts

Seeds of apples, pears, and oranges

Kernels inside the pits of peaches, apricots, plums, and cherries

Stems or leaves of tomatoes

Any green parts of a potato

Long ago, identifying plants was confusing. People sometimes got mixed up about whether a plant was safe to eat or not. People also used plants for medicines, so learning to identify plants became very important. In the 1700s a scientist named Carl Linnaeus (lin AY uhs) created a way of naming plants and putting them into groups. His system helped people quickly identify plants. It made him famous, too. Scientists still use his system today.

Chapter 5
DESERT WONDERS

The cactus is known as a desert plant. Every part of a cactus helps it survive in the hot, dry desert. It stores water in its trunk and branches, which are tough and waxy to keep the plant from losing moisture. Sharp spines all over the cactus serve a double purpose. They protect it from wind and sun. They also defend it against animals looking for a meal or a drink of water.

Desert soil is thin, and it drains quickly. Cactus roots have adapted to this soil. The shallow roots spread out through the thin soil. As a result, the roots soak up a lot of water during short desert rainstorms.

Most people agree that of all the cactus trees, the saguaro (suh WAHR oh) is number one. Because of its size and shape, people have given the saguaro many names. For example, it's been called a prickly horror and a plant with a personality.

A saguaro is a tree, but it grows so slowly that it doesn't reach 20 feet (6 meters) for almost 100 years. Most other trees grow much faster. It takes almost 75 years for the saguaro's branches, or arms, to appear. By the age of 150, the saguaro is about as tall as a three-story building.

Saguaro cacti in Arizona

The saguaro's flowers bloom in the spring. Creamy white and bowl-shaped, these flowers bloom only at night. About 100 flowers open on each tree during a month. Insects, birds, and bats pollinate the saguaro flowers. The long-nosed bat stops for a drink of nectar during its long **migration** north from Mexico. Some birds peck holes in the trunk and branches to make a nest for their family. They make new holes every spring. Then other birds take over the old nests.

The saguaro's prickly fruit ripens in the summer. Each fruit is plum-sized and holds as many as 2000 tiny seeds. Coyotes, foxes, squirrels, wild pigs, and other animals eat the fruit and its seeds. One tree may produce up to 40 million seeds during its long life. Only three or four of those seeds will become trees. People have also used the fruit from the saguaro tree. American Indians knocked them down with long poles so that the thorns wouldn't cut them. They used the bright red pulp of the fruit for jams and syrups and fed the seeds to their chickens.

The saguaro's home is in the Sonoran Desert of Arizona. About 50 other kinds of **cacti** live there, too. Like the saguaro, many of them have fruits that make tasty jams and candies.

Some cacti have interesting names that suggest what they look like. For example, the hedgehog cactus has long spines that resemble the thick prickles of a hedgehog. This plant tends to be just a few inches tall. Hedgehog cacti are also known for their beautiful blossoms that come in a rainbow of colors.

Barrel cacti look like barrels full of water. In fact, these plants have soft, spongy tissue inside. Their pulp does not offer a refreshing drink, but a bitter mouthful. Teddy bear cholla looks like a furry critter, but this type of cactus is the prickliest of all! Organ pipe cacti have clusters of large stems that suggest huge organ pipes. Unlike the saguaro, these trees have no separate trunk.

Organ pipe cacti

Teddy bear cholla

Chapter 7
MEAT-EATING PLANTS

The purple top of a pitcher plant shines in the sun. The plant's nectar gives off a sweet smell. A fly moves into the tube of the plant, looking for nectar that lies under the hood.

The fly doesn't know it has made a huge mistake. The tube of the pitcher plant is an insect trap. Its surface is slippery, with hairs pointing down. The fly lands and then slides into the liquid at the bottom. The liquid is deadly, and eventually it dissolves the bug. It's dinnertime for the plant!

There are about 600 kinds of **carnivorous** plants. Like the pitcher plant, most carnivorous plants eat insects. Some trap tiny fish and other small water creatures. Sometimes a bird, mouse, or frog may be eaten, too. Carnivorous plants attract insects the same way other plants do. They have inviting colors, smells, and patterns.

Pitcher plants

Some carnivorous plants have a sticky goo that catches an insect as soon as it lands. Some, like the pitcher plant, are slippery inside. Other meat-eating plants have trap doors that push in. Once a little creature has entered, it's trapped! Some meat-eating plants, such as the sundew, have traps with moving parts. These parts may curl around the insect or grab it tight. The door will not push back out. The most famous trapper of all is the Venus flytrap. The leaves of this plant look like open clamshells with thorns along the rim. When an insect lands, the leaves slam shut.

The next step is for the plant to kill its prey. Some plants, like the pitcher plant, do the deed by drowning it in a strong liquid. This liquid dissolves the soft parts of a trapped bug. Soon the bug parts become a rich soup. Then the plant can absorb its meal.

Why do carnivorous plants need meat? Carnivorous plants grow in swamps and on mountainsides where the soil lacks minerals that most plants need. Meat-eating plants get these minerals from the creatures they trap.

The hairs of the sundew plant make a sticky liquid that attracts insects.

Chapter 8
FOOD PLANTS

A plant called cacao (kuh KAY ow) is the plant from which we get cocoa and chocolate. Long ago, the Maya and Aztec people of Central America found that a rich drink could be made from ground-up beans of the cacao plant. Cacao beans became very valuable. At one time cacao beans were thought to be so valuable that they were even used as money.

Real money doesn't grow on trees, but over time humans have discovered just how important and valuable plants are to health and survival. Corn, potatoes, and peanuts are among the world's most valuable crops. Corn grows on stalks above ground. The kernels we eat are the plant's seeds. Potatoes grow in the ground. But potatoes aren't seeds or fruits. They are the swollen parts of underground stems. Potatoes are actually the plant's stored food. Even though peanuts are called nuts, they are not real nuts. True nuts—like walnuts—have tough, thick shells. Peanuts are seeds that grow inside soft pods. Peanut plants have flowers with **shoots** that tunnel into the soil. Pods grow from these shoots.

About 6000 years ago, people of Central and South America learned to grow corn. These early farmers also grew beans, squash, tomatoes, pumpkins, and peppers. **Agriculture** allowed early people to settle down and form villages. In contrast, ancient hunters were always on the move. They had to follow their main source of food, the animal herds. Farming people, such as the Maya, created farms and cities because they needed to stay put and tend their crops.

By the 1500s many Spanish explorers had arrived in Central and South America. They were searching for gold and silver. On their return trips to Spain, they brought back crops from the Americas, including corn, potatoes, peanuts, cacao beans, peppers, squash, and tomatoes. Soon Europeans tried growing these new foods at home. By the late 1500s, Spanish farmers sold potatoes at markets in Spain.

By the 1700s potatoes were the main food of the people in Ireland. Large amounts of potatoes could be grown on little land. In 1845 a potato disease ruined Ireland's crop. Many Irish people starved or left the country.

People have grown corn for thousands of years. Many towns in the Middle West of the United States built corn palaces in the late 1800s. Some towns still do. These palaces show the region's prized corn crop and are covered with odd-colored corn.

Corn has a never-ending number of uses. Cereal, soft drinks, chips, syrup, **margarine,** ketchup, shaving cream, soap, wallpaper, and even plastics are made from corn. Corn is also used in things like batteries, paint, magazines, shoe polish, and twine.

A corn palace
in South Dakota

About Potatoes

- Some people used to eat potatoes with other foods to help stomachaches.

- Potatoes were so expensive in the 1600s that they were only eaten by wealthy people. Later they became a very cheap food.

About Peanuts

- Some American Indians buried peanuts with the dead so that they wouldn't be hungry in the afterlife.

- About 2 billion pounds (4.4 billion kilograms) of peanuts are eaten in the United States each year. Peanut butter makes up half this amount.

- Peanut shells have been used to make kitty litter.

- Peanuts are also used to make shoe polish, shaving cream, ink, cosmetics, soap, and paint.

About Corn

- Each American eats about 14 gallons (53 liters) of popcorn each year.

- Some American Indians built floating corn gardens on the tops of rafts.

Glossary

adapt (uh DAPT) to adjust or change to fit an environment

agriculture (AG rih kuhl chuhr) the science or business of farming

broadleaf (BRAWD leef) **trees** trees with flat leaves

cacti (KAK ty) more than one cactus; plants that have needles and grow in hot, dry places

canopy (KAN uh pea) the uppermost leafy level of a forest

carnivorous (kahr NIV uhr uhs) meat-eating

conifers (KAHN uh fuhrz) cone-bearing trees

environment (ehn VY ruhn muhnt) the natural conditions that make up an area in which a plant, animal, or person lives

fragrant (FRAY gruhnt) having a pleasant smell

margarine (MAHR juh rin) a soft food spread used in place of butter

medicinal (mih DIS uh nul) used to treat, prevent, or cure diseases or relieve pain

migration (my GRAY shuhn) the act of moving from one place to another at a certain time every year

minerals (MIN uh ruhlz) solid natural substances found in the earth, such as salt or iron

nectar (NEK tuhr) a sweet liquid found in flowers that attracts birds and insects

photosynthesis (foh toh SIN thuh sis) the process by which green plants use light to change water and carbon dioxide into food for themselves

pods (PAHDZ) soft shells that contains seeds

pollen (PAHL uhn) small grains that contain the male cells of a plant

pollination (PAHL uh NAY shuhn) the process by which pollen moves from a plant's male parts to a plant's female parts

predators (PRED uh tuhrs) animals that hunt and eat other animals

reproduce (ree pruh DOOS) to create more of a species

shoots (shoots) growths that come from a plant

species (SPEE seez) a group of plants or animals with common features that set them apart from others

Index

Acacia tree 18, 20–21

Baobab tree 16, 18–20, 21

Barrel cactus 30

Bristlecone pine 13

Broadleaf tree 11, 14–17

Bromeliad 10

Bucket orchid 9

Cacao plant 34

Conifer 11–13

Corn 34, 35, 36, 37

Darwin, Charles 21

Durian tree 16–17

Dwarf willow tree 21

Foot-and-a-half orchid 8

Giant sequoia 12, 13

Gingko tree 21–22

Hedgehog cactus 30

Kapok tree 16

Linnaeus, Carl 26

Mangrove tree 16, 18–19

Maple seed 16

Milkweed 24–25

Mirror orchid 8

Monarch butterfly 24–25

Oak tree 14–17

Organ pipe cactus 30

Peanut 34, 35, 36

Photosynthesis 4

Pitcher plant 31, 33

Poison ivy 24, 25

Pollination 7–9, 21

Potato 34, 35, 36, 37

Saguaro cactus 27–29, 30

Sundew 32, 33

Teddy bear cholla 30

Titan arum 5–6

Upas tree 23

Venus flytrap 32